D0098931

Donated by
Fred & Bev Durst
2008

PHINEAS L. MACGUIRE . . .

For Jack Dulaney Dowell,
Future Vulcanologist and Astronaut

—F. O. D.

Other Books by Frances O'Roark Dowell

Chicken Boy • *The Secret Language of Girls* • *Where I'd Like to Be* • *Dovey Coe*

Atheneum Books for Young Readers • An imprint of Simon & Schuster Children's Publishing Division • 1230 Avenue of the Americas, New York, New York 10020 • This book is a work of fiction. Any references to historical events, real people, or real locales are used fictitiously. Other names, characters, places, and incidents are products of the author's imagination, and any resemblance to actual events or locales or persons, living or dead, is entirely coincidental. • Book design by Sonia Chaghatzbanian and Michael McCartney • The text for this book is set in GarthGraphic. • The illustrations for this book were rendered in pencil. • Manufactured in the United States of America • First Edition • 10 9 8 7 6 5 4 3 2 1 • Library of Congress Cataloging-in-Publication Data • Dowell, Frances O'Roark. • Phineas L. MacGuire . . . Erupts!: the first experiment / Frances O'Roark Dowell. — 1st ed. • p. cm. • Summary: Fourth-grade science whiz Phineas L. MacGuire is forced to team up with the new boy in class on a science fair project, but the boy's quirky personality causes Phineas to wonder if they have any chance of winning. • ISBN-13: 978-1-4169-01957-2 • ISBN-10: 1-4169-01957-7 • [1. Schools—Fiction. 2. Science—Experiments—Fiction.3. Friendship—Fiction.] I. Title. • PZ7.D75455Fro 2006 • [Fic]—dc22 2005012605

THE FIRST EXPERIMENT

rupts!

by FRANCES O'ROARK DOWELL • illustrated by PRESTON McDANIELS

Atheneum Books for Young Readers
New York London Toronto Sydney

SCIENCE

chapter one

My name is Phineas Listerman MacGuire.

Most people call me Mac.

It's okay if you call me Phin.

You can even call me Phineas.

Forget about calling me Listerman.

I am allergic to fifteen things. My mom says this is not true, that I'm only allergic to two things, peanuts and cat hair. But I am a scientist, and she's not. I have scientific proof that it makes me itchy to think about the following items:

Avocados
Yogurt, any flavor
Cottage cheese
Grape jelly
Any kind of kissing,
especially when there's lipstick
Celery
Purple flowers
Purple Magic Markers
Purple crayons
Anything purple
Moist towelettes in foil packs
Telephone calls
All girls

I started fourth grade three weeks ago. When I started, I had a best friend.

His name was Marcus Ballou. Marcus is also a scientist. We were a scientific team. We specialized in volcanoes, caves, fossils, all insects, and the solar system. But mostly volcanoes.

We have made and erupted over eighty-seven volcanoes in our lifetime. It's very simple. You take an empty soda bottle (big) and put it in a baking pan (also big). Fill the bottle with lots of baking soda and four or five squirts of dishwashing liquid.

Then add vinegar and stand back.

You should do it outside, in case you were wondering. Unless you have a less irritated mom than mine. Then maybe you could do it on the kitchen table. If you're like me and spill stuff everywhere even when you're trying really hard to be careful, you should definitely do it at a friend's house.

Here is the problem with Marcus: He moved. To Lawrence, Kansas. This is bad for at least two reasons. Now we aren't a scientific team anymore. Also, he waited until the second week of school to move. If he had moved before school started, then I would have known to look around for a new best friend on the first day.

But I didn't know to do this. I still had Marcus.

Everybody knew that me and Marcus were best friends and a scientific team. No one else tried to be best friends with us. They picked other best friends.

Here's what you would hear all the time:

"Mac and Marcus"
"Mac and Marcus"
"Mac and Marcus"

Now all you hear is:

"Mac"
"Mac"
"Mac"

Scientifically speaking, it's a pretty lonely sound.

FROG
JAR

chapter two

I do not have a best friend. I do have an un-best friend.

Here is the weird thing: His name is also Mac. Mac Robbins, known as Mac R. in our class, since we have two Macs. He moved here this year from Seattle, Washington.

The first day of school our teacher, Mrs. Tuttle, made the three new kids stand up in front of the class, one at a time and say a few words about themselves. Two of the kids shuffled their feet and said where they used to live and stuff like their hobbies were playing on their Game Boys and watching TV and their favorite class was lunch.

Mac R. did not shuffle his feet. He looked everybody straight in the eye and said, "I am from Seattle, Washington. Everything is better in Seattle, including the ice cream, the road signs, and the television shows."

Then he said children from Seattle, Washington, are naturally geniuses. He said children from our state are not.

"Quite a first impression, Mac R.," Mrs. Tuttle said when Mac R. was done making everyone in our class automatically hate him. She took one of the rubber frogs from the rubber frog collection she keeps on her desk and put it on her head to put us in a better mood.

It didn't work. We still hated Mac R. And it got worse. The next day he tripped Chester Oliphant on his way to the pencil sharpener. Chester is the size of a kindergartner, but he's the funniest kid in our class, so everyone likes him and sticks up for him out on the playground. He is the wrong person in our class to pick on.

Mac R. said it was an accident, but nobody believed him. Marcus, who only had three days left at our school before going to Lawrence, Kansas, said having Mac R. in our class almost made him glad he was moving away.

Two days after that Mac R. wore a Woodbrook Elementary School T-shirt, only he'd put a big red circle around the school logo and then a slash through the circle. It was like he wished our whole school didn't even exist.

We felt the same way about him.

When I first heard there was another Mac in the fourth grade, I was interested from a scientific angle. I had never met another Mac before. I wondered if we would look anything alike. Maybe we would dream about the same things at night. Maybe we would have the same habits, such as drawing on our bedroom walls with Chap Stick (the picture shows up about two weeks later, when enough dust has stuck to the Chap Stick wax) or waiting three months to empty the trash can in our room so that any thrown-away, half-eaten snack foods, like bananas or grapes, have decomposed into a pile of slimy goop.

Here's what I know now: We do not have one thing in common.

Mac R. is short, with stick-out brown hair and freckles. He picks his nose when he thinks nobody is looking.

I'm tall for my age. I only pick my nose when I know for sure nobody is looking.

Mac R. loves dinosaurs. He's in love with them. He has a DINOSAURS OF THE CRETACEOUS AGE lunch box and three dinosaur T-shirts—stegosaurus, iguanodon, and triceratops—that he wears over and over. Marcus and I liked dinosaurs back in preschool, mostly when we were three-day threes and four-day fours, and maybe a little bit in kindergarten. In first grade we gave up dinosaurs completely.

Okay, maybe sometimes I take out my supersize T. rex and let it stomp on my LEGOs. But only once in a while.

And I'm not in love with it.

The funny thing is, once I started thinking about things I have in common with other people, I realized that I didn't have everything in common with Marcus, either. We both love science and performing scientific experiments, and we both have dads who are teachers. Only, Marcus lives with his dad, and my dad lives two hundred miles away from me. Marcus collects baseball cards, and I collect dried worms (I want to win the world record for the longest dried earthworm ever recorded, but I will probably have to move to Australia, where they have the world's longest worms, to actually do this).

Marcus is neat. At the end of third grade I won the awards for Messiest Desk and Person Least Likely to Comb His Hair Before Coming to School in the Morning (my teacher made up that award especially for me). Marcus loses his temper and yells at people and then isn't mad at all five minutes later. Frankie Wasserman punched me in the nose in first grade, and I still want to sock him one every time I see him.

Today at lunch the person I have nothing in common with, Mac R., sat at my table. It's the table for people who don't have anyone else to sit with. Mason Cutwelder was there, setting up his little green army guys to attack Roland Forth's peanut butter sandwich. Roland Forth sat across from him. He hummed. Roland Forth is always humming. It's like having a radio going all the time when you're in the same class as Roland Forth.

I sat at the other end of the table, reading *Scientific American*, which is an important magazine that all scientists read, even if they don't understand all the vocabulary.

I was reading the letters to the editor when Mac R. plopped his tray on the table next to me. We had picked exactly the same things from the cafeteria line, except his Jell-O was green and mine was red. And mine had milk sloshed all over it from when I accidentally knocked over my milk carton with my copy of *Scientific American*.

No one looked up when Mac R. sat down. Part of sitting at the table for people who don't have anybody else to sit with is pretending no one else exists.

I don't know why that makes sitting there less bad, but it does.

Mac R. didn't know the rules of sitting at this table. He started talking immediately. He said that when his permanent records arrived at Woodbrook Elementary, we would know for sure that he was the smartest boy in Mrs. Tuttle's class, and the whole fourth grade. His permanent records would be official proof.

Roland Forth stopped humming for a second. "But probably a lot of the girls are smarter. Girls are always the smartest."

Roland Forth is the only boy in the fourth grade who would point this fact out.

For the most part, other boys don't like Roland Forth.

Mac R. frowned. He said, "There are no smart girls."

He probably should have said that more quietly.

"What do you mean there are no smart girls?" Aretha Timmons leaned over from her lunch table and gave Mac R. the evil eye. "Everybody knows girls are the smartest ones. There's scientific proof."

My ears got all tingly when I heard the words *scientific proof*. When you're a scientist like me, you're always on the lookout for scientific conversations. You won't find many in the cafeteria of Woodbrook Elementary.

Mac R. stuffed a roll in his mouth. "Girls are stupid. They play with dolls. They wear pink shoes."

Aretha stuck out her foot. Her shoe was a navy blue sneaker with silver stripes.

It was not pink.

"Mrs. Tuttle doesn't wear pink shoes either," Aretha said. "You don't know very much, do you?"

Mrs. Tuttle wears green high-top shoes every day. She says they make her bouncy, like a frog. All in all, Mrs. Tuttle would be a very good teacher, except that she wears too much purple. It doesn't match her yellow hair or her green shoes.

Also, it makes me itch just to see it.

"Mrs. Tuttle is different," Mac R. said. "She's a teacher. Teachers have to be smart. Besides, she's a grown-up. She's not a girl."

Aretha marched over to our table and pointed her fork at Mac R. He jumped back in his seat, like he was afraid she was going to poke him.

I could tell she wasn't going to poke him. She just wanted to make a point.

"I'll prove it that girls are smarter than boys," Aretha said. "Or at least that I'm smarter than you. I'm reading on the sixth-grade level, for one thing."

Mac R.'s face turned red. You could tell he didn't read on the sixth-grade level.

"For another thing, I'll beat you at the fourth-grade science fair in two weeks," Aretha said. She put her fork back on her tray and smiled.

Aretha is the only person I know who is as excited about the fourth-grade science fair as I am. She is also my only serious competitor, at least in Mrs. Tuttle's class.

I wonder what project she'll do.

I wonder if she likes volcanoes.

I wish girls didn't make me itch.

chapter three

My mom did a scientific experiment this morning.

She didn't mean to.

"These beans have been in here at least a month," she said, pulling a plastic container out of the refrigerator. "How did they get pushed way in the back?"

My mom is always trying to get us to eat more beans. She says they're healthy. The problem is, everyone in my family would rather eat pizza.

Including my mom.

I ran over to where my mom was standing. "Is there any mold on them?"

I am scientifically very interested in mold.

"Nope," she said, prying off the blue lid. "But they've been in the fridge so long we probably shouldn't eat them. I'm going to throw them away."

Five seconds after the lid came off, the kitchen started filling with a strange smell. It was like everybody in the world had farted at the same time.

As a scientist, I found this very interesting.

"Open the windows, quick!" my mom yelled. She ran to a window in the living room and started tugging at it.

It wouldn't open.

She tried the other living-room window.

It wouldn't open either.

This is how we found out all the windows in our house are stuck closed.

My mom was pretty upset. She had to leave for work in fifteen minutes, and she was afraid that the bean smell would still be there when she got home. She didn't like the bean smell. Even worse, she didn't think the women in her book club would like the bean smell either.

"Eight people will be here at seven PM and it's going to smell like every toilet on the street backfired," she moaned. She rubbed her forehead, like she suddenly had the worst headache in the world.

"Mom?" I said.

"Not right now, Mac," she said, waving her hand at me.

"But Mom."

"I mean it, Mac," my mom said, sounding irritated. "You need to run and catch your bus. Your lunch money is in your backpack."

It's very easy to irritate my mom. Marcus could do it by just walking in the front door. He never knocked, and the first thing he did when he came in was yell "Hello!" at the top of his lungs. He didn't care if my sister was napping or if someone was on the phone or anything.

My mom cared.

When you have grown up with an irritated mother, you know when to leave her alone. I grabbed my backpack off of the kitchen table and left for the bus stop. I felt pretty happy. I had needed something for Share and Stare, and now

I had something. Even better, it was a scientific something.

Share and Stare is Mrs. Tuttle's version of Show and Tell, in case you were wondering. You have to show something or talk about something that has to do with a school subject, like math or science or books. I think she's afraid that fourth graders would think regular Show and Tell is for babies.

She's pretty right about that.

"So you see," I told my classmates at the end of my Share and Stare turn later that morning, "my mom shouldn't worry, because the gas molecules—that's what was stinking up our house, the gas from the beans—will have broken apart long before tonight, and our house won't stink anymore."

I thought everyone would be interested

in my story. What I didn't realize was that some people would be interested in the wrong way.

"Hey, Stinkazoid," Mac R. called on the playground. "Remind me never to come over to your stinkoid house, okay?"

I was sitting on a swing, looking at a volcano book that Marcus had given me before he moved. Reading this book made me feel sad. There were two reasons:

1. It made me miss having a best friend, and
2. It made me realize I was sort of losing interest in volcanoes.

"I mean it," Mac R. called. "I'm going to stay three miles away from your house at all times. Pee-yew!"

"Good," I told him, hardly bothering to look up from my sad volcano book. "I was hoping you'd say that."

I heard somebody laughing like my comeback had been really good instead of just okay. "Big Mac attack!" Aretha shouted from the monkey bars. She ran over to the swing and slapped high fives with me. Then she turned to Mac R.

"You shouldn't talk so much about stinking, Stink Bomb!" she yelled.

You could tell Aretha hadn't forgotten

Mac R.'s remarks about boys being smarter than girls.

My hand stung a little bit from slapping high fives. I didn't mind, though. Me and Marcus used to slap high fives all the time. That's how we celebrated our many scientific breakthroughs.

Slapping high fives with Aretha made me feel better. And my hand didn't even itch. I walked back to room 34 feeling like it was going to be a good rest of the day.

Which shows you how much I knew.

chapter four

"Listen up, team," Mrs. Tuttle yelled. "Time to zip your lips."

She made the zipping sign by pulling her fingers across her mouth. A bunch of kids did the same thing and started making funny buzzing noises, like they were trying to talk through their zipped lips.

This made Mrs. Tuttle learn her lesson that "zip your lips" is more of a little-kid thing. This is her first year of teaching fourth grade after three years of first-grade teaching. She's still getting adjusted.

Here is what makes Mrs. Tuttle a good teacher: Instead of yelling at us some more about being quiet, she made the buzzing noise back at us. Then she skipped through the room singing, "I am the Bee of Silence, beware my sting!" and poked the buzzers in their arms. It helped people get the silliness out of their system, and we all quieted down.

"Fourth-grade science fair," she said, writing it on the board. "We've talked about it, we've

dreamed about it, and now the time has finally come."

I pounded my fists on my desk so it sounded like a drumroll, which is what guys do instead of jumping up and down in their seats and screaming when something the teacher says makes them happy, which is what girls do. The fourth-grade science fair is the first time you can be in a science fair at our school. Me and Marcus had been practicing science projects and experiments for the fourth-grade science fair for years. Some of our greatest hits included:

1. Exploding film canisters. You fill a film canister halfway with water, drop half a tab of Alka-Seltzer in it, put the top back on, then move out of the way—the

cap pops off and flies into the air like a rocket ship. This is an experiment about gas buildup, although not the kind that stinks up your whole house.

2. Microwave marshmallows. Put a marshmallow on a paper plate and zap it for thirty seconds. The coolest part is when the marshmallow gets really huge and looks like it's going to explode. The second coolest part is how it stays white on the outside but gets all toasted on the inside. It's like the opposite of roasting marshmallows over a campfire.
3. A cannibal insect study. There are many insects that eat their own kind, including

praying mantises (sometimes), lacewing larvae (if there's nothing else around to eat), cannibal mites (which actually aren't insects, but everybody thinks they are, so we counted them), and pirate spiders. The only problem with this study was that it made us stop liking these insects after we thought about them awhile. I mean, eating your friends and relatives is a pretty gross thing to do.

Remembering all our great experiments, I couldn't believe that Marcus wasn't here, now that it was finally time to prove to the world what great scientists we were. Years from now would anyone at this school even remember that Marcus had always gotten hundreds on his science tests? That in second grade me and Marcus had been famous for capturing seventeen tadpoles in the creek behind Marcus's house and donating the whole jar to Mrs. Hinkle's class?

I guessed I would just have to win the fourth-grade science fair for the both of us.

Ideas for projects started bouncing around in my head. I wouldn't mind doing something that exploded and had lots of smoke and sparks, something with a Bunsen burner and a chemistry set. I've been begging my mom to buy me a Bunsen burner and a chemistry set since I was seven, but she says that people like me, people who never saw a glass they didn't automatically knock over, should not be allowed in the same room with chemistry equipment.

Mrs. Tuttle held up a clipboard. "Sign-up sheet. You need to work with a partner. Whoever doesn't have a partner, please raise his or her hand."

Four kids raised their hands: me, Mac R., Roland Forth, and Aretha Timmons. I was surprised that Aretha didn't have a partner, until she said, "Mrs. Tuttle, do we have to have a partner? My idea for a project won't work very well with two people."

"Sorry, Aretha," Mrs. Tuttle said. "That's the rule this year."

Aretha shook her head like she couldn't believe how stupid having partners was. "It's not fair," she muttered, and popped her pencil on her desk a few times.

"It's good to collaborate, Aretha," Mrs. Tuttle said. This is a big word with teachers, I've noticed. I had never thought about how they were always making you work in groups and pairs, until I didn't have an automatic partner. Now I am thinking they should just be quiet about all this collaborating and let some people work by themselves sometimes.

I was working up my nerve to tell Mrs. Tuttle that I would be Aretha's partner. I knew that if I said that, people would say I wanted Aretha to be my girlfriend. They would say this very loud and for a long time.

I didn't want people to say this. I didn't want them to yell "Mac loves Aretha!" when I got on the bus in the morning. I didn't want them to yell "Hey, Mac, there's your girlfriend!" every time Aretha walked into room 34.

The only thing worse than everyone

yelling about Aretha being my girlfriend would be having to do a science fair project with Mac R. or Roland Forth.

"Roland!" Mrs. Tuttle called out. "You and Aretha partner up. And please stop that humming."

Aretha's pencil popped even harder on her desk. Roland pulled his desk close to hers. He didn't stop humming even for a second.

"And that leaves the two Macs," Mrs. Tuttle said, writing something down on her clipboard. "You guys pull your desks together and do some brainstorming. Everybody get together with your partners. I want a description of your project—in stunning, multicolor detail—by Monday. Research project or experiment, take your pick."

Here's what surprised me: Mac R. actually seemed excited that we were going to be partners. I thought he would

be as mad as Aretha. But he dragged his desk over to where mine was right away, bumping into about eight other kids on the way.

"High fives, big guy!" Mac R. said when he sat down. He lifted up his right hand for a big high-five smack.

This was the same hand he'd been using to pick his nose with all through journal writing. He had had a dictionary in front of his face, but I could see his finger jabbing in and out.

I did not high-five Mac R.

He changed his high five into a kind of wave, but when I turned around to see who he was waving at, all I saw was the art supply closet.

Mac R. leaned toward me. He seemed to have forgotten about me being a stinkazoid person. "I've got one word for you," he said.

I closed my eyes. I knew what was coming.

When I opened my eyes, Mac R. was grinning.

"Dinosaurs," he said. "Amazing, incredible, fantastizoid dinosaurs."

"That's five words," I told him. "Unless you only count *dinosaurs* once, and then it's only four words. Plus, I don't think *fantastizoid* is an actual word."

Mac R. waved away my word count. "We can do something really awesome,

I just know it. Maybe something with raptors. Maybe we could build one that really flies."

I put my head down on my desk. "How do you build a dinosaur?" I asked, not bothering to look up. "A flying one, which has to be done in two weeks?"

"You get a kit, moron."

I lifted up my head a few inches and looked at Mac R. "You can't use a kit for a science fair project."

This didn't seem to concern him at all. "You just throw away the box," he said. "Nobody would even know it was a kit."

"They would know. Even if they aren't automatic geniuses like people in Seattle, Washington, the judges would know. My sister would know, and she doesn't know anything about science at all."

Mac R. pounded his fist against his desk. He was even more excited than before. "Hey, I saw you reading about volcanoes on the playground. We could do raptors flying around a volcano, and the volcano could explode!"

"Erupt," I said. "Volcanoes do not explode. They erupt."

I may be the world's biggest milk spiller, but I am not sloppy when it comes to scientific terminology.

"Whatever," Mac R. said. "A volcano would be awesome."

I didn't want to do a volcano, and I especially didn't want to do a volcano with Mac R.

But I had a feeling that was exactly what I would be doing.

chapter five

This morning, after I'd watched Saturday cartoons, I sat at the kitchen table and brainstormed some alternate science fair project ideas. Here's what I came up with:

1. When you drink milk and start laughing, why does the milk automatically squirt out of your nose? Does only milk from a little

MILK
banana peels
rotten eggs
under wear
elly beans
What Makes
Mold ?

carton do this? How about milk from a glass? From a plastic cup? If you were drinking a juice box, would stuff still come out of your nose, or does juice automatically go straight to your stomach?

2. Why do rotten eggs stink? How long does it take an egg to get rotten? What would happen if I put an egg under my bed with all the unwashed socks and underpants and empty potato chip bags and banana peels and all the black and pink jellybeans from every Easter basket I've ever had? Would the egg turn rotten faster than if it were stashed somewhere halfway clean?

3. What makes mold? What stuff gets the moldiest? Why is the cheddar cheese in our refrigerator always moldy?

The more I thought about number three, the mold idea, the more interested I got. And then I had an amazing scientific breakthrough. What if I brought our refrigerator to school for my science project?

Our refrigerator is practically a museum of mold. We should ship it off to a science lab where they're trying to come up with cures for diseases. Penicillin is made from mold. Who knows what they might discover after studying our fridge for a few weeks?

Here's what happens: My mom does the grocery shopping on Saturdays. She brings home about ten bags of very healthy food and about two bags of stuff my family will actually eat. The healthy food gets pushed to the back of the refrigerator or stuffed into the produce drawers.

Every week my mom piles on a new layer of healthy food. This goes on for three or four weeks, until (a) there is no more room in the refrigerator and (b) something starts to stink really bad. Then it's time to clear out the fridge and start over. This is the best time to look for mold.

You should start in the dairy drawer. Our cheese gets moldy the fastest. There are probably four or five plastic-wrapped chunks of moldy cheddar cheese in our refrigerator any time you open the door. And it's amazing how much mold will grow on feta cheese that comes in a container. It's also amazing how much feta cheese stinks even before it gets old and moldy.

I won't even discuss the cottage cheese situation.

Next you should look at all the opened cans on the top shelf. There is a very interesting black mold that grows in tomato paste, for example. Don't forget to look at any open cans of soup. Soup grows mold that looks like little stars.

I was taking mold notes in my science journal like crazy. And then I thought: *Big Mac Double Attack! Magnets on the outside, mold on the inside.* I would take down all the junk our fridge magnets were holding up, mostly notices for PTA meetings from last year, and once I got everything down, I could put up interesting information about magnets. I would use magnets to hold up all this interesting information, of course.

I wasn't quite sure how I would convince my mom and stepdad to let me take the refrigerator to school. Well, I knew I couldn't convince my mom, but sometimes my stepdad could be reasoned with.

First, though, I would have to reason with Mac R.

I was supposed to go to Mac R.'s house at four. Actually, it wasn't a house, it was an apartment three streets away.

Marcus's house had been three streets away in the other direction. On

Saturday mornings I would ride my bike to his house or he would ride his bike to mine, and we would watch cartoons and make plans for new volcanoes and other interesting scientific investigations.

I started getting that sad feeling again, thinking about Marcus. I was getting a little tired of that feeling, if you want to know the truth. So instead of sitting around thinking about how bad it was not to have a best friend, I hopped on my bike and rode to Mac R.'s place. I would share my great scientific ideas with him. I could bring him back to my house and show him all our refrigerated mold. Maybe I could convince him that mold was about a trillion times more interesting than dinosaurs and volcanoes.

Just thinking about mold made the sad feelings go away.

If you need cheering up, a little mold will do the trick.

When you're riding your bike really fast, your brain starts going pretty fast too. From the time I left my house until the time I got to Mac R.'s apartment, about a thousand ideas went through my head. More and more of these ideas started being about how much I didn't want to do my first really important science project on little-kid things. I was supposed to be a scientist, not a kindergarten teacher. My job wasn't to do something just because Mac R. wanted to do it. I was in the business of making scientific breakthroughs. Dinosaurs and volcanoes were not in the scientific-breakthrough department.

By the time I got to Mac R.'s apartment, I pretty much wanted to punch him in the mouth.

"What are you doing here?" he asked when he opened the door. He was wearing Spider-Man pajamas, and his hair was sticking out even worse than usual. He looked like he was a very tall two-year-old, if you want to know the truth.

"One word," I told him, holding up a finger, which I thought about poking him in the chest with, just to let him know I meant business. I probably would have if he hadn't looked like such a preschooler.

"T. rex?"

"Officially speaking, *T. rex* would be two words," I said. Looking past him into the apartment, I saw he had cartoons on the TV, and not the public-television

34

cartoons, which were the only ones my mom let me watch at home. "Can I come in, by the way?"

Mac R. looked nervous. "I'm not supposed to have anyone over when my mom's at work. That's why I told you to come at four. That's when she gets off."

"Where does she work?" I asked.

"She's the manager of the apartment complex," Mac R. said. He poked his head out the doorway and looked left and right. "I guess you could come in for a few minutes. But if my mom calls, don't answer the phone."

Scientifically speaking, I was starting to think it was highly unlikely Mac R. was the smartest fourth grader at Woodbrook Elementary.

I mean really highly unlikely.

chapter six

"Mold? You want to do a science project about mold?"

Mac R. fell back against the couch. He looked a little green.

"Yes," I told him. "Mold is very scientific. And it's everywhere, in my refrigerator, under the wall-to-wall carpet, and blowing around in the air. You've heard of mold spores, right?"

Mac R. looked even greener. "I

thought we were going to do a volcano."

"I remember you said something about volcanoes the other day, but this mold idea came to me from out of nowhere. I think we could win first place with it. It's a much better idea than a volcano."

"Do you really think your mom will let you take your refrigerator to school?" Mac R. asked.

I shrugged. "I think my stepdad could talk her into it if he felt like it. He does this thing where he tickles her and says funny stuff, and after about five minutes of that she usually gives in."

Mac R. stared at the TV. It didn't look like he was watching it, though.

"My dad's still in Seattle," he said. "We moved here after my parents got divorced."

Now it was my turn to stare at the TV. It's hard to know what to say when people tell you terrible stuff about their lives. I probably should have said something like maybe one day he would end up with a nice stepdad like I did, which doesn't automatically make your parents getting a divorce okay, but it does make the day-to-day stuff a little better.

I didn't say that, though. I can never think of the right thing until about four hours later.

Mac R. turned and looked at me. "The thing is, I was already sort of working on the volcano plan. Do you want to see what I've done so far?"

Not really, I felt like saying, since I'd already decided a volcano was a dumb idea. But you can't be rude two seconds after someone tells you the worst thing in his life, so I followed Mac down the

hallway and into the bedroom at the very end. He flipped on the overhead light. "This is my room," he said. "I'm supposed to clean it before I watch any TV, but I haven't gotten around to it yet."

Mac R.'s room looked like it had been picked up, turned upside down, and shaken all around until it rattled.

I was impressed.

He started tossing things all over the place. "Okay, now let me just find that notebook," he muttered. "It's here somewhere. Maybe it's under the bed—no,

no, here it is. Okeydokey artichokies, take a look at this."

He handed me a sketchbook opened to a picture of a volcano. "Did you draw this?" I asked. Mac R. nodded.

It was the best drawing of a volcano I'd ever seen in my life. Every single detail looked exactly real. I shook my head. "You're an artist. You're probably the best artist of the fourth grade."

"I'm not an artist," he said. "Boys can't be artists. I just like to draw."

"What do you mean boys can't be artists?"

Mac R. took the notebook back from me and closed it. "My dad says boys can be architects, they can go into graphic design, or they can be advertising art directors. But they can't be artists, because art is for girls."

"No offense," I said, "but your dad's

wrong. My uncle Conrad is an artist. He draws comic books. He did paintings of me and my sister that look exactly like us. He's an amazing artist."

Mac R.'s eyes lit up. "He draws comic books? Because that's what I want to do." He got down on his hands and knees and pulled a box from under his bed. It had about two million sketch pads in it.

"I'm working on a comic book now,

as a matter of fact," he said, handing me one of the sketch pads. "It's called 'Derek the Destroyer.' It's about a guy who flies around at night stopping crimes and destroying evil stuff."

I looked at a couple of pages. Mac R. was not only an excellent drawer of volcanoes, he could also draw comics. I'm not a big comic-book reader, even though my uncle Conrad is always trying to get me interested in them. But I could tell Mac R.'s were good.

I noticed something at the end of one of the stories. It was a little signature in the corner of the last box. "Who's Ben?" I asked.

Mac R. turned red. "That's me."

"Is that your comic-book artist name?"

"No," he said. "That's my real name. Mac is my middle name." He picked up a robot action guy that was on his bed and twisted its arms into different positions. "Well actually, Peter is my middle name. Nobody calls me Mac except for people at school."

I sat down on the bed. "Why? I mean, our class already had a Mac. It's not like we need another one."

Mac R. had gone back to his normal color for a few seconds, but now he was redder than ever. "It's stupid. I don't even know why."

"There must be some kind of reason."

"I just like the name Mac, okay? You don't own it, you know. It's not your real name either. You're really Atticus or Maximus or something."

"Phineas," I said. "I'm named after my great-great-uncle. He was an inventor and played baseball for the Cleveland Indians' single-A team, and one time he went over Niagara Falls in a barrel."

"What did he invent?"

"This kind of gum that had cloves in it, for people with toothaches," I said. "And some other stuff too. But the gum was his most famous thing."

Mac R. grabbed his comic book back. "Gum's stupid."

"So's telling everybody your name is Mac when it's not really your name. That's about the stupidest thing I can think of."

"I know it's stupid!" Mac R. stood up and glared at me. "Don't you think I know it's stupid? You're the one that's stupid if you don't think I know it's stupid to tell people that your name is Mac just so you'll have one stupid thing in common with somebody in your class."

I was thinking it was possible that

Mac R. was the most confusing person I'd ever met in my whole life. But I decided not to say this. I thought maybe it was time to not have this conversation anymore. Maybe we could start a conversation that didn't have so much yelling in it. I said, "So should I start calling you Ben? I mean, it's a good name and everything."

All the sudden Mac R. looked tired, like he'd just run a hundred miles. "Yeah," he said, sitting back down on the bed. "It's starting to feel really weird that nobody in this school calls me Ben."

I looked some more at Mac R./Ben's comics. He was a genius, that was for sure. Just not a school kind of genius.

"Do you just want to do pictures of volcanoes for our project?" I asked him.

"No, these are just design ideas. I was

thinking we could get some plaster and some sculpey clay. It would be pretty easy to build a model. We could put some drawings on a board, too, maybe to show the inside of the volcano, stuff like that."

I nodded. This was actually a good plan. It was sort of getting me interested in volcanoes again. I could make some posters that explained how volcanoes worked and told some facts about the really famous volcanoes, like Mount Saint Helens and the volcanoes in the Ring of Fire.

"Do you know how to make a volcano erupt?" I asked Mac R./Ben. He shook his head no.

"Then, I'll be in charge of that," I told him. "It's too bad we can't build a real volcano, like a miniature one. But the lava's around two thousand degrees Fahrenheit or something. It's just this big mass of molten rock charged with gas, and it breaks through the earth's crust, which is totally hard to do. Lava is like the Superman of nature, if you know what I mean."

Mac R./Ben nodded again, like he knew exactly what I meant.

And then he put up his right hand and we slapped high fives.

The word *boogers* never even crossed my mind.

chapter seven

Here are some weird facts about what happened after that:

1. My brain had no problem making the switch from Mac R. to Ben. I think this was because I didn't like Mac R. and I did like Ben. So my brain sort of forgot that Mac R. ever existed.

2. I started playing with dinosaurs again. Or at least I took them out when Ben came over to my house for lunch, after we kind of, sort of, halfway straightened his room so his mom wouldn't go ballistic when she saw it. When we got to my house, my mom had just come home from the store and was stuffing some doomed spinach into the refrigerator.

"I thought you said you didn't like dinosaurs anymore," my mom said when I told her I needed the step ladder to get the box of dinosaurs down from the top shelf of my closet. "I thought that was a Let-it-Go box."

A Let-it-Go box is one where you put stuff that you don't play with anymore but aren't quite ready to send to Goodwill. What happens is that you sort of forget about it, and then one day you look in your closet and the box is gone and you can't remember what was inside it in the first place.

"I guess I'm not ready to let it go yet," I said. I could tell this answer did not make my mom happy. She's very big into decluttering. Every few weeks you hear her on the phone saying, "I can't believe what a mess it is in here. Time to declutter!" It's the most cheerful you will ever hear my mom sound.

She sighed an irritated sigh. "Okay," she said. "You can get it down." Then she turned to Ben. "Do you like dinosaurs?"

Ben nodded. My mom sighed again and looked at me. You could tell she thought I'd made a crummy choice when I picked

Ben for my new friend. A re-clutterer. That's like a crime to my mom.

My dinosaur collection isn't all that great, if you want to know the truth. Partly that's because I stopped collecting dinosaurs in kindergarten, and partly it's because Marcus borrowed a bunch of my dinosaurs and didn't actually return them. So now most of my dinosaur collection is living in Lawrence, Kansas.

Here are two things I learned about Ben that afternoon:

1. He is not only a drawing genius, he is also a dinosaur genius.

He knows every fact there is to know about dinosaurs, and he's pretty good at telling you these facts without making you want to jump out of your window just so he'll shut up.

2. He's really a pretty nice person. I realized this when he acted like my dinosaurs were very interesting and worthwhile, when in fact, two of them have spent time in the microwave, four of them were left outside on the deck for three years in all sorts of weather conditions, and the rest of them have been pretty well chewed on by my dog, Schmitty, and my little sister, Margaret.

I wondered how a pretty nice person like Ben could have spent the first month of school acting like the pretty-not-nice person Mac R. And then I wondered if the other people in our class would ever give him a second chance. He had made a big mess out of the first one, you had to admit.

"Are you going to tell everybody that your name is Ben?" I asked him as we were putting the dinosaurs back into the Let-it-Go box. "I mean, at school next week? Because they might like you if you were Ben. They still think you're Mac R."

Ben tossed a stegosaurus from hand to hand. "I wish Mac R. had never been born," he said.

"Me too," I agreed. "He was really irritating."

Ben sighed and looked at me. "Do you ever get in an obnoxious mood, and you know you're being obnoxious, but you just can't stop?"

I nodded. I'm like that when my cousin Allen comes to visit. Separately me and my cousin Allen are both sort of quiet and prefer scientific thinking to stuff like wrestling and chasing other people around with sticks. But if you put us in the same room, watch out. It's like a chemical reaction we have to each other.

"It's probably too late to make friends with anybody but you," Ben said. "I think I blew it with the rest of our class."

If you're a scientist like me, you're always interested when a problem comes around. Because what you learn when you study science is that if you think hard enough and are willing to take risks, almost every problem has a solution.

It's just a matter of discovering what that solution is.

"Don't worry," I told Ben. "I'll think of something."

And you know what? About five minutes later I did.

WOODBROO

chapter eight

I met Ben in front of the school first thing this morning. "Did you get everything done?" I asked him.

Ben nodded and dropped a paper bag at my feet. We'd spent most of Saturday night and all of yesterday coming up with a plan for reintroducing Ben to the kids of Mrs. Tuttle's class. The ideas were mine, but Ben had to do most of the actual work. Of course, I had to write up our volcano plans for Mrs. Tuttle, so we were even.

"I didn't make as many copies as you said," Ben told me as we walked toward the door. "My mom wouldn't let me use the copier in her office, so I had to go to the library, and the library copier sort of exploded before I got finished."

I was automatically jealous. The most exciting thing I'd ever seen at the library was when this kid got his arm stuck in the outside book return and his mom started yelling for someone to call the fire department. The head librarian finally came outside with a toilet bowl plunger and unstuck him.

"Did it *explode* explode?" I asked. "Did you get burned? Did they take you to the hospital?"

Ben pushed through the door, dragging his bag behind him. "Well, maybe it didn't explode exactly. But there were definitely sparks. And smoke. Really bad-smelling smoke."

"Electrical fire," I said. "That's the worst-smelling smoke, next to burning hair. My sister Margaret's hair caught on fire last year when she was blowing out her birthday candles. Talk about stinkazoid."

Ben turned around and grinned. "You learned that word from me," he said. "I use that word in my comic books all the time. I'm pretty sure I made it up."

We were the first kids in school. That was part of the plan, to corner Mrs.

Tuttle before anyone else got there and get her okay for what we wanted to do.

"Ben, huh?" Mrs. Tuttle said after we'd explained the situation to her. "I've been wondering why you decided to use a nickname in class, especially since your mom referred to you as Ben instead of Mac when she came to Parent Open House night."

Mrs. Tuttle leaned back in her seat, giving Ben the big once-over. She chewed thoughtfully on the end of a purple pen she'd been using to grade papers when we walked in.

"Why don't you use red ink like other teachers?" I asked her. I was starting to feel itchy thinking about homework papers covered in purple ink.

"Red is a nervous-making color for some people," Mrs. Tuttle explained.

"They see a lot of red ink on their paper, it stresses them out. Purple, on the other hand, is a soothing color."

"Not to me, it isn't," I said, scratching my arm. "I'm allergic to purple."

"Do you actually break out in hives when you come in contact with it?" Mrs. Tuttle wanted to know, sounding interested.

"Practically," I told her. "It's pretty bad."

"Well then, I'll use red on your paper. You're not allergic to red, are you?"

I shook my head no. Mrs. Tuttle smiled. Then she told us we were welcome to try out our plan at Share and Stare, but not to get our hopes up too high. "No offense, Ben," she said, "but it can be hard to undo first impressions."

"And my first impression was a pretty bad one," Ben admitted, slumping back against the chalkboard. "My second and third ones too."

Mrs. Tuttle handed Ben a red rubber frog from her desk drawer. "Why don't you hold on to Felix today? He'll put the spring back into your step."

Share and Stare was right after math. Mrs. Tuttle does math first thing every morning because she says it pumps up the brains of all the math people in the class and gets it out of the way for the nonmath people. I personally am a math person, so I started Share and Stare in high-octane Big Mac Attack mode. Usually I'm the sort of person who stays halfway in his shell, more observing than making a lot of noise about everything, but when I'm in Big Mac Attack mode, watch out.

"Ladies and gentlemen," I announced first thing, "only moments ago, without anyone noticing, I made someone in this class disappear. Look around you and see who's missing!"

It surprised me how long it took for somebody to figure out it was Ben. He'd slipped out of the room a few minutes before, when Mrs. Tuttle was showing the class her fake poisonous rubber frog named Lester, the latest addition to her frog jar.

Finally Melissa Beamer figured it out. "Where's Mac R.? If he's the one you made disappear, I hope he's gone for good."

A bunch of kids clapped. I noticed that Aretha Timmons clapped loudest of all.

MRS TUTTL

"Yes, that's right," I said. "I made Ben—I mean, Mac R.—disappear. And for my next trick I am going to replace him with someone much, much better."

"Who?" everyone in the class asked at once. "Who?" It sounded like a gigantic owl had just flown into the room.

"A practically famous artist," I told them. "In fact, this artist has been observing our class for several weeks now, and I have some of his artwork to share with you."

I pulled Ben's bag from behind Mrs. Tuttle's desk and took out a stack of stapled papers. "There aren't enough to go around, so you'll have to share with a buddy," I said. Everybody automatically turned to the person to their right, except for the kids on the farthest right row, who automatically turned to their left. Mrs. Tuttle is very big on buddies. She brought this habit over from the first grade.

At least she doesn't make us hold hands when we're walking to the playground.

As soon as people got a look at the handouts, they got very quiet. There were four sheets stapled together, copied front and back. You could almost hear people concentrate as they looked

at the pictures and read the words. I walked over to Aretha's desk and looked over her shoulder. She was staring at a picture of herself.

"Who did this?" she asked me. "Who drew this picture? It looks just like me, or what I'd look like if I lived in a comic book."

It was true. You could have looked at that picture cross-eyed and upside down and still have known it was Aretha.

All around us people started talking. They were saying, "Did you see the picture of me?" They told one another their superhero names, which were written under their pictures.

Ben had done a comic book of our class. That was my great idea. Because everybody loves to see pictures of themselves. And everybody likes people who

can draw. It's practically a rule that if you can draw, people will want to be your friend. In third grade there was this girl in my class named Emily Porter who could draw great pictures of horses.

Everybody was always asking Emily Porter to draw them a horse. They completely ignored the fact that she cheated on spelling and math tests, and you had to cover up your paper if she sat anywhere near you.

After people had had a chance to point out their pictures to everyone, I clapped my hands to get their attention. "Would you like to meet the artist of this brilliant document?" I asked them. They all nodded.

I walked to the door and opened it. Ben was waiting outside in the hallway. He looked very, very nervous.

As a matter of scientific fact, he looked like he might throw up any second.

"Ladies and gentlemen, may I introduce to you the world's greatest artist, Ben Robbins!"

When Ben walked into the room, he was squeezing Felix so hard I couldn't help but be glad that Felix wasn't real. Frog guts all over the floor might have made everyone forget about Ben's great art.

"Ben?" somebody yelled out. "That's not Ben! That's Mac R."

Somebody booed.

Mrs. Tuttle walked over to Ben and put her arm around his shoulder. "Maybe you'd like to do some explaining now, Ben?" she said. Ben nodded.

That's when he told everybody that he knew he'd been a jerk and he was sorry he'd said a bunch of obnoxious things at the beginning of school. He also told them that he wished they would call him Ben instead of Mac R.

"I'm tired of being a Mac," he said. He turned to me. "No offense."

I wasn't offended. I was tired of him being a Mac too.

Two seconds later Ben was mobbed. Everybody wanted him to sign the comic book he'd drawn of our class. People wanted him to sign the cover and by their picture. Michelle Lee, who'd been in the same third-grade class as me, wanted to know if Ben knew how to draw horses.

I sat down at my desk, feeling satisfied. Using sound scientific reasoning, I had come up with a plan to make people like Ben, and looking around the room, I could tell my plan had worked. You could tell that people had already forgotten Mac R. completely and thought Ben was great.

Well, maybe not everyone had forgotten. Behind me I could hear the sound of a pencil popping against a desktop. It was a very mad-sounding pencil. I turned around slowly.

"Maybe he can fool everybody else into believing he's changed," Aretha Timmons said, glaring at me. "But I know better. That boy will always be Mac R. to me."

chapter nine

I think I have mentioned the fact that I'm allergic to girls. My mom says you can't actually be allergic to other human beings, but she's wrong about that.

Here is my scientific reasoning: A person can be allergic to animals, right? When this happens, it's usually because of their dander. If the word *dander* reminds you of dandruff, that's because it's just like dandruff. It is flaky skin that comes off and gets into the air and into people's noses.

Which is kind of gross if you think about it for too long.

If you are allergic to an animal's dander, you will spend a lot of time sneezing your head off if you get near that kind of animal. Your skin will also start to do weird things. Once I did this experiment where I touched a cat on purpose, and then I videotaped the hives coming out on my arms. It was really cool.

Until they started to itch.

They itched for three hours.

It was a pretty stupid experiment, if you want to know the truth.

People's skin flakes off all the time. My mom won't let my stepdad wear anything black or dark blue because he has dandruff like snowflakes falling from his head.

I'm not allergic to my stepdad's dander, but theoretically I could be. Dander is dander, is the way I see things. And if I could be allergic to my stepdad, I could be allergic to girls. Maybe most girls have extra-flaky skin, and that's why they make me itch so bad.

Since I'm allergic to girls and am not friends with any girls, you wouldn't think that I'd care about Aretha Timmons's opinion. I should just try to stay away from her the way I stay away from peanuts and cat hair.

But the fact is, Aretha Timmons is my only fellow scientist in Mrs. Tuttle's fourth-grade class. There are some other kids who get As in science like me and Aretha, but that doesn't automatically make them scientists.

Once, Aretha asked me if she could look at my copy of *Scientific American* when I was done reading it. She wanted to read an article about DNA.

Later, when I asked her if she had understood it, she said she had understood about 25 percent.

Which was 24 percent more than I had understood.

Also, I have noticed that Aretha gets very excited when we start a new science unit. Her eyes sort of light up and she pops her pencil hard on her desk. It's happy popping, like she's ready for the show to get on the road.

For some reason I've never felt allergic to Aretha. Maybe in an alternate universe we'd be friends, working together in a lab, wearing white lab coats with our names stitched across the front pocket.

In this universe, though, we aren't getting along too well.

The second we finished saying the Pledge of Allegiance this morning, I felt Aretha's pencil pop on my shoulder. When I turned around, it was like she'd never stopped glaring at me from the day before.

"You are going to lose at the science fair big-time," she told me. "I'm going to stomp you and Mac Two into the ground."

"His name is Ben," I said. "And he's not as bad as you think he is. He was

just going through an obnoxious stage right when he moved here."

It felt good to stick up for Ben. That's one of the coolest things about being friends with somebody. You stick up for them, they stick up for you. Like the time last year James Long accused Marcus of stealing his idea for a science report, and I dumped my lunch tray on his head. That felt really good, watching the sloppy-joe junk slide down his nose, especially since I got away with it. I am always dumping my lunch tray on somebody, only usually it is an accident.

"Just because it turns out he can draw doesn't mean he's so great," Aretha said. "I'm sad to see he's got you fooled just like all the rest of them, though. Anyone can see that he's just using you for your scientific knowledge.

When it's time for the science fair, he's just going to pull you down. You're going to lose for sure."

I tapped my fingers on my desk. I didn't want Aretha to hate me just because she hated Ben. On the other hand, I didn't think her behavior was very scientific, either. "Where is your evidence that he has me fooled? How do you know that you're right and I'm wrong? What data have you collected? What experiments have you run?"

Aretha shook her head. She popped her pencil sadly on her desk. She sighed and said, "I've got the evidence that's in front of my own eyes. I've got three weeks of observed behavior. You've got a comic book." She looked at her pencil for a minute, like maybe it would tell her why I'd made the huge mistake of becoming friends with Ben, then she stuck it behind her ear. "Well, I guess that's just less competition for me at the science fair."

I turned back around. All the sudden I wished that Marcus was still there, so we could be doing the science fair together. Because Aretha was probably right; when you added me and Ben together, we didn't make some great scientific team that you'd be reading about in books someday. What you got was a good scientist and a really good artist. Together that didn't automatically add up to first place at the fourth-grade science fair.

It had never occurred to me before that I might not win first place at the fourth-grade science fair.

It was occurring to me now.

But I was pretty sure Aretha was

wrong about Ben. I didn't think he was using me for my great scientific brain. I wanted to prove she was wrong, but I didn't know how.

I guessed that would have to be up to Ben.

Getting our science fair project started would definitely be up to me. I rode my bike over to Ben's apartment after school for a brainstorming session. It was hard to get him in a scientific mood, though. He had a notebook full of drawing orders placed by people in our class.

"Are they paying you?" I asked him.

Ben shook his head. "No. This is my plan for getting people to like me again."

"You mean to like you for the first time," I said.

"You could put it that way," Ben said. "But I like the way I said it better."

I took out my science journal, ready to get down to business. If we were going to have a chance at winning first prize at the science fair, we didn't have a minute to waste. "Okay, the way I see it, we need to plan the building of the volcano, the construction of the landscape around the volcano, the erupting of the volcano, and the use of any multimedia materials that the judges might give us extra points for. You definitely need to draw some cross sections of a volcano so people can understand what the inside looks like, before lava starts flowing and after it starts flowing."

"No prob," Ben said. He held up a picture of Michelle Lee's dog. "They sort of look the same, don't you think?"

"Who looks the same?" I asked, looking up from my journal.

"Michelle and her dog," he said. "I mean that in a good way."

I held up my journal and waved it in the air. "Hello, are you planning on helping with this project or not?"

"I'll help, I'll help, don't get all stressa-zoid on me," Ben said, scratching his ear

with his pencil while he studied the picture of Michelle Lee's dog. "I'll take care of the whole volcano business. My mom got me a piece of plywood to build it on. All you have to do is draw me a diagram for the inside of the volcano. You can be in charge of all the big-brain stuff, like the writing part."

That sounded like the less fun part to me, if you want to know the truth. But Ben was an artistic genius and would build an amazing volcano. I can make a volcano with a soda bottle, but I can't even make a paperweight out of clay.

I opened my journal back up and started drawing volcano diagrams for Ben. "I'll get my mom to buy us a plastic tube to put the vinegar and baking soda in, for the eruption," I said. "You'll need to build around that. What we're trying to demonstrate here is that lava can overcome gravity and be pushed through the earth's rock crust. Since we can't actually use real lava, we kind of have to create a simulation, using the gas created by the baking soda and the vinegar. . . ."

Ben wasn't paying attention to anything I said. He held up his drawing of Michelle's dog. It looked exactly like the photo, except it had artistic style to it now.

"That dog really does look like Michelle," I said. "It's sort of amazing."

Ben smiled. "Next I'm doing a drawing of Roland Forth's Chihuahua. The two of them are practically twins."

Maybe that could be our science fair project next year, a study of why people look like their pets. My brain started getting very excited about that idea. Some of that excitement went right into my pencil, and I actually did some really good volcano drawings for Ben to use when he started to build the volcano. I was amazed by how good they were, if you want to know the truth.

That's the great thing about science, in my opinion. It will make you excited about everything in the world.

chapter ten

I thought the week before the science fair would be pretty ordinary. Ben and I would work on our project in the afternoons. I would do my other homework at night. My mother would be irritated by 95 percent of the things that happened to her on a daily basis, and my stepdad would order take-out food three nights in a row, even though every week he and my mom say they are going to quit ordering takeout and do real cooking.

But this has turned out to be one of the weirdest weeks I've had all year. Here is what happened.

On Monday my nose started bleeding in math. There were big splotches of blood all over my desk. It looked really neat. Mrs. Tuttle sent me to the school nurse, who is a man named Joe Martinez. In kindergarten everybody was sort of scared that we had a man nurse, but now we're all used to it.

"Let me show you something, Mac," Mr. Martinez said while I sat in his office with an ice pack on my nose. He typed something into his computer, and up came a picture of the inside of a nose.

"What you're looking at is a picture of the anterior septal blood vessels," Mr. Martinez explained to me, pointing at the picture. "That means the blood vessels in the front part of your nose. This time of year your nose gets dried out; it's not uncommon to have a nosebleed or two."

Then he swiveled around in his chair and looked straight at me. "When I was your age, I did a lot of nose picking. Kids around nine, ten, eleven, are notorious nose pickers. Just ask Mr. Reid."

Mr. Reid is our school's janitor. "How does Mr. Reid know?" I asked.

"Who do you think has to clean all those boogers off the bottoms of your desks at the end of the year?" Mr.

Martinez asked. "If anybody knows anything about fourth-grade nose picking, it's Mr. Reid."

"That's a pretty cruddy job," I said.

Mr. Martinez nodded. "Yeah. But I know you're not the kind of kid who'd put a booger under your desk, are you?"

I shook my head. I am a completely private nose picker. No picking at school is pretty much a rule I live by.

"Here's the thing, Mac. Keep the picking to a minimum. It really irritates your nose. This time of year it's hard to keep your finger out of your nose. I'm sympathetic to that. But you don't want to bleed to death for a bunch of mucus, now do you?"

My face was a little red by the time I left Mr. Martinez's office. But I haven't picked my nose since.

The second weird thing that happened was the art supply closet in Mrs. Tuttle's room got haunted. We've been in school over a month now, and that closet hasn't made a peep. But all the sudden, on Wednesday morning, a *knock, knock, knock* sound came from the back of the room.

Everyone said, "Huh?" and turned around to look at the same time. All that's back there is a sink, some cabinets, and the art supply closet.

Knock, knock, knock, the sound came again. No doubt about it, it was coming from the art supply closet.

"Open it up, Mason," Mrs. Tuttle called from the front of the room. "Maybe Picasso got locked inside and is trying to get out."

"No way," Mason said. "I'm not opening that thing." He turned to Brandon

Woo, who sits right next to him. "You open it."

Brandon shook his head no. All along the back row people were shaking their heads like, *Don't look at me.*

Finally Mrs. Tuttle walked over to open the door. The people in the back row leaned as far away from the art supply closet as they could. The door squeaked when Mrs. Tuttle tugged on it, then it flew open.

A paintbrush fell out. About seven different people screamed.

I couldn't believe what I saw.

Absolutely nothing.

chapter eleven

The art supply closet was completely empty.

Normally you would have seen about two million things. Stacks of drawing paper, construction paper, tracing paper, and colored squares of felt. A whole shelf of paint and an army of paintbrushes. Pipe cleaners, Popsicle sticks, toothpicks, and a big plastic bag of clay that Mrs. Tuttle was always

telling us not to let get dried out or else it would just be a big plastic bag of brick.

And on the very bottom shelf of the art supply closet you would have seen a pink papier-mâché pig that nobody had any idea of how it got there. Not even Mrs. Tuttle.

"What in the world?" Mrs. Tuttle said. "Where did all my art supplies go?"

Brandon Woo picked something up off of the floor. "Here's the paintbrush that fell out," he said, handing it to Mrs. Tuttle.

Mrs. Tuttle stared at the paintbrush, like if she looked at it hard enough, it might tell her what in the world was going on. After a minute she shook her head, closed the art supply closet door, and said, "Okay, sports fans, I'm going to make a quick check at the principal's office to see if any other mysterious disappearing acts have been reported this morning. Talk quietly among yourselves until I get back. Absolutely no hanky-panky."

"It's a ghost," Stacey Windham said the second Mrs. Tuttle left the room. She sounded like she was the world's biggest expert on supernatural happenings in art supply closets. "What else could it be? Besides, my sister was in this classroom last year, and she said that somebody died in here a long time ago."

"I heard that too," said Mira Ligotta, who is Stacey's second best friend, after Lori Birch. "It was, like, five years ago. My neighbor who's in eighth grade told me about it once."

"How'd they die?" somebody asked. People all around the class were scootching their desks closer to Stacey and Mira.

Lori Birch, who you could tell did not like Mira taking center stage next to Stacey, leaned into the circle of desks. "Their babysitter? She put poison in their tuna fish sandwich. Nobody knew what was going on. The class came back from lunch, and this kid just fell down and died."

"It wasn't their babysitter," Mira insisted. "It was their stepmom."

Lori rolled her eyes. "Whatever."

I looked around the room. Some kids were definitely starting to look like they were having second thoughts about eating lunch that day. Then I saw Aretha. You could tell she didn't believe a word of what was being said.

"So if I go online and do a search about a poisoned kid dying at Woodbrook Elementary School, I'll be able to find all the details?" she asked, sounding very doubtful.

Stacey shook her head. "They kept it a big secret so that the school wouldn't get sued."

"Why would the school get sued if somebody's babysitter poisoned a student?" I asked. "It's not the school's fault."

"I'm sorry, Mac," Stacey said sweetly. "I didn't know you were a lawyer with all sorts of legal facts in your brain."

Aretha snorted. "Mac is just using

logic, which is more than I can say for you people."

Just then Mrs. Tuttle burst back into the room. "Mystery solved! Well, almost solved, anyway." She walked to the front of the class. "It turns out that when Mr. Reid was cleaning the room last night, he noticed paint dripping from the closet. When he opened the doors, sure enough, several paint jars had been overturned and had spilled—which means some of you aren't putting the lids back on tightly enough, by the way. So anyway, he took everything out to clean the closet, and then he took the stuff downstairs to get the paint off."

"How did the paint get spilled in the first place?" I asked. I was an expert at spilling stuff, but I couldn't figure what could have knocked the paint jars over while they were still in the closet.

"Hmmm," Mrs. Tuttle said. "I'm not sure. Maybe someone was playing back there and bumped into the shelves?"

Everyone turned and looked. The shelves looked pretty sturdy. It would take more than a kid bumping into them to shake them.

"The ghost did it," Stacey said in a loud whisper. "How obvious can it be?"

"What's obvious is that you have peanut butter for brains," Aretha said, then turned to Mrs. Tuttle. "There must be some logical explanation. Something in that closet spilled that paint, and something is making that thumping noise."

"I'll tell you what," Mrs. Tuttle said, taking a yellow frog out of the frog jar and pulling on its leg. "I will give extra credit to the person who can solve this mystery. Plus this frog."

"We'll need to see the stuff from the art supply closet," Aretha said. "That might give us some clues."

"You'll only make the ghost mad," Stacey said. "He'll probably come over to your house to haunt you."

Aretha ignored her. Mrs. Tuttle said that anyone who was interested in solving the mystery could go to Mr. Reid's room at lunchtime and examine the evidence. We could also spend as much time as we wanted looking inside the art supply closet.

When lunchtime rolled around, me, Aretha, and a few other kids went to Mr. Reid's room in the school basement. He was in there eating a turkey sandwich and reading the sports page. We told him why we were there, and he led us to a table with all of Mrs. Tuttle's art supplies.

"I wasn't able to save all the paper," he told us. "But everything else is cleaned up. In fact, when you're done examining it, you can take it back to Mrs. Tuttle's classroom."

I picked up a paint jar and looked at it carefully. Could gases have built up inside it and caused it to explode all over the closet?

But what would explain the noises in the closet even after all the art supplies had been moved out of it?

"Mr. Reid? Do you still have the paper you couldn't save?" Aretha asked. Mr. Reid led her to a big trash can in the corner of the basement.

You know how sometimes people talk about a light going off in their head? I've never actually had that happen to me, but sometimes I get this feeling that's almost like electricity. This happens when a big idea practically knocks me over.

I knew exactly why Aretha wanted to look at that paper.

chapter twelve

"Teeth marks," I said as Aretha pulled the paper out of the trash. "Look for teeth marks."

She nodded. "And ripped-up paper. For a nest. I bet if we look hard enough, we can find a nest, or at least the beginnings of a nest."

We dug through the trash together. It was kind of a mess down there, since a lot of the paper had paint on it. I checked my shirt. It was a halfway-nice, almost-new striped T-shirt. I predicted five minutes of yelling from my mom if I got paint on it.

For my mom five minutes of yelling really isn't that much.

I kept digging.

Aretha was the one who pulled out a sheet of red construction paper that had been gnawed on. A few seconds later I pulled out what looked like green and yellow confetti.

We looked at each other.

"Mice," we said at the same time.

Mrs. Tuttle would be very impressed by how fast we had solved the mystery. But who would get the extra credit? I wondered. Aretha had gotten the idea about five seconds before I did, but we both found the evidence together. If I'd been the one to have the idea first, I would have shared the extra credit with Aretha.

But now that Aretha hated my guts, I wasn't so sure she would share extra credit with me.

"Brilliant!" Mrs. Tuttle exclaimed when Aretha told her our findings. "Now all we have to do is set a humane trap, and we'll send our little mouse friend back to the woods first thing in the morning. And I'll mark down extra credit for Aretha right now."

I turned to go to my desk. I didn't really need extra credit anyway, I told myself. But I guessed it would be nice to get a *little* credit.

"Mrs. Tuttle," Aretha said. "Mac

should get half of the credit because he was half of the team who solved the mystery."

I looked at Aretha. She looked at me. She didn't smile.

I was pretty sure she still hated my guts.

But that didn't mean she wasn't an honorable person.

"Extra credit for you both!" Mrs. Tuttle exclaimed. "But who gets the frog?"

"Aretha should get the frog, since she came up with the idea it might be a mouse first," I said.

"Fair enough," said Mrs. Tuttle, and she tossed Aretha the yellow frog. Aretha pocketed it, then sat down.

That afternoon Ben and I put the finishing touches on

our science fair project. We had pretty much taken over Ben's dining room. His mom didn't care. She likes to eat on a tray while she's watching TV. First, though, she puts on her pajamas and a pair of fuzzy pink slippers.

Ben's mom is not like other people's moms.

"If Aretha thinks she's going to beat us, she's got another think coming," Ben said as he painted a stream of lava flowing down the volcano.

"We don't even know what she's doing," I pointed out. "She's been very top secret about it. For all we know, she's cloned her cat."

"Still wouldn't be as cool as this baby," Ben said.

I had to admit, the volcano did look pretty cool. Even though it was just sitting there, it gave you the feeling it could erupt at any minute. And all the details of the stuff around it—the grass, the trees, the rocks—made you feel like you'd stepped through a time machine to a real place. A very small place, but still an actual real, live place.

I reached into my backpack and

handed Ben a piece of paper. "Here's the checklist for everything you and your mom need to bring in the morning," I told him. Ben's mom drove a pickup truck. It was very handy for transporting science fair projects.

Also, I have a bad habit of forgetting stuff. Like the time last summer my dad took me and my sister to the beach for a week and I forgot to pack my swim trunks.

And my goggles and my Boogie board and my beach towel.

Since then I've gotten pretty good at making lists, but it's still a good idea to put somebody else in charge of checking them twice. Especially when the list is about something as important as the fourth-grade science fair.

The funny thing is, my mom and

Ben's mom almost got in a fight over who would drive the project to school. My mom may be irritable, but she'll drive you to school in a second if you've got a project. It's because when she was a kid, this one time she had to carry this clay owl she made for homework on the school bus, and she tripped getting on. The owl's beak got smushed and both wings flopped off. So she's very sympathetic about getting stuff to school all in one piece. That's why she called Ben's mom a couple of days before the science fair and told her she would take our project.

I was eating crackers on the couch on the other side of the room, but I could still hear Ben's mom getting all upset on the phone because she'd gotten someone to work for her so *she* could take the project. My mom told me later she could tell how much Ben's mom just wanted to do this one important thing for Ben.

My mom can actually be a very understanding person when she feels like it.

Ben took the list I'd handed to him and let it fall to the floor. I walked around the table and picked it up.

"I'm serious, Ben," I said. "Mrs. Tuttle says we only get fifteen minutes to set up our project. If we forget something, there won't be time to run home to get it."

This time Ben took the paper and shoved it in his jeans pocket. "I won't forget," he promised, dipping a brush into a jar of green paint and touching up a tree.

"Don't forget," I said.

"I told you, I won't," Ben said.

Scientifically speaking, I was pretty nervous that he would. So on my way out I taped another copy of the checklist to his fridge and one on the front door.

When you're dealing with artists, it's a good thing to plan ahead.

chapter thirteen

The second I walked into the fourth-grade science fair, I had this feeling like maybe I was the dumbest person on the planet. Which is not a good feeling when you are planning to be a world-famous scientist one day.

I had to walk from the entrance of the cafeteria all the way to the far back corner to get to my exhibit, so I got to look at all the different fourth-grade

SCIENCE FAIR

science fair projects. As soon as I saw an experiment about sulfurous water, I knew picking a research project over an experiment project had been a huge mistake on my part.

Do you know what sulfur smells like? Like the worst thing in the world. Rotten-egg horrible. Supreme skunk stinkazoid.

It smells great.

When I thought about how I could have spent the last two weeks making stinky sulfur water in the bathtub, I felt terrible. I had gotten carried away about volcanoes when I saw what an artistic genius Ben was. Geniuses can be very persuasive people. That doesn't make them the best people to choose your science fair topic, however.

The second reason I felt so dumb was

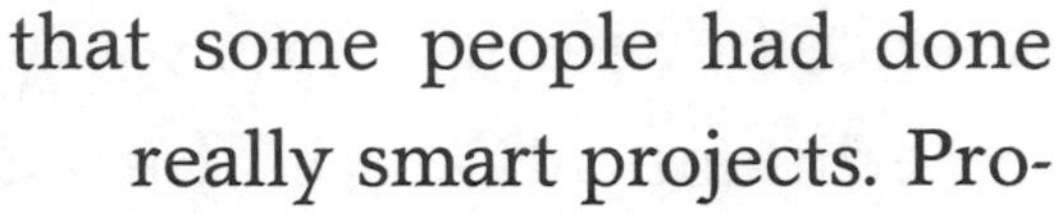

that some people had done really smart projects. Projects that made volcanoes and dinosaurs look like stupid, little-kid stuff. Joe Smelts and Will Rajhaheed had rigged up a doorbell system with a battery, a switch, some wire, and a buzzer. Everybody was lined up to push the button, like they'd never rung a doorbell before. It was just cool to see one that someone you knew had built.

One of the coolest projects I saw was a tape recorder that had been taken apart so you could see how it worked. This kid had pulled out the tape heads so he could run a strip of cassette tape across them using his hand. He was recording people's voices and then playing them back, sometimes fast, sometimes slow, sometimes backward, which sounded supremely weird.

You would think, with computers and the other technology we have today, hearing your voice on an old cassette player wouldn't be so fascinating, but it was.

Walking across the cafeteria and looking at these projects, I had two billion ideas for other scientifically brilliant projects. Which made the fact I'd done a research project on volcanoes even harder to live with.

The last thing that made me feel dumb was when I saw Aretha's project. This was easy to see because her table was set up right next to mine.

Aretha and Roland had set up a spy laboratory.

DISAPPEARING INKS
& Spy Glasses
SECRET
CODES
HOW A
MAGNIFYING
GLASS WORKS

They had made three kinds of invisible ink for writing spy notes—lemon juice, baking soda, and cornstarch.

They had written a secret code and built a decoder device that fit onto a wristwatch.

They'd made spy binoculars out of paper towel rolls and magnifying glasses.

On the wall behind them were posters telling you about all the scientific facts of their spy lab. Like how magnifying glasses work and the recipes for invisible ink and the chemical reactions that make each ink work.

On the table they had samples of invisible ink for people to try.

They were the hit of the fourth-grade science fair.

It could have been me.

If I weren't allergic to girls, I could have been a science star.

Instead I was just some dumb kid who still played with dinosaurs.

chapter fourteen

I was almost ready to go throw myself into a vat of day-old spaghetti sauce in the cafeteria's kitchen, when something caught my eye.

It was the most awesome volcano I'd ever seen. And maybe it wasn't a real volcano, but it sure looked like it could be real, if volcanoes were only ever two feet tall.

I'd seen that volcano before; in fact,

I'd seen it every day for the last week. But somehow it looked different at the science fair.

For the first time I saw how other people would see it.

It was a genius volcano.

"Do you think the ankylosaurus is in the right place?" Ben asked when he saw me. "Or is it too close to the volcano? It might gross people out if the ankylosaurus bites the big one when the volcano explodes."

"Erupts," I told him for the zillionth time. "Volcanoes don't explode, they erupt."

"Whatever," Ben said, adjusting the dinosaur's position. "I just don't want to get personally blamed for the extinction of the dinosaur."

There are two parts to the science fair. The first part is where people walk around and look at all the projects. The second part is when the judges walk around. When the judges walk around, both people on the team have to be seated at their table to tell the judges about their project.

This year's judges were the school principal, Mrs. Patino; the sixth-grade science teacher, Mr. Marks; and the school nurse, Mr. Martinez.

Me and Ben were waiting until the judges got to our table to erupt our volcano. We felt this would give our project a little extra oomph. When the judges were three tables away, I reached under the table for our eruption supplies—baking soda, vinegar, and dishwashing liquid for extra eruption action.

It was all there. Except for the vinegar.

"Where's the vinegar?" I asked Ben. I stuck my head under the table for a second look.

"It's down there," Ben said. He sounded a little unsure, though.

"Did you check it off the checklist?"

"Of course I checked it off the checklist. Why wouldn't I check it off the checklist?"

This time he sounded very unsure.

I sat back up. "Because you forgot to check the checklist?"

"I guess that could be one reason," Ben agreed. "But boy, doesn't this volcano look great?"

That's when Aretha leaned over from the spy lab. "Is there a problem over here, boys?"

She sounded sort of happy about the idea, if you want to know the truth.

"We're fine," I told her.

"I forgot the vinegar," Ben told her. "I meant to check the checklist, but I sort of slept late this morning. It was pretty crazy just getting everything over here on time."

"No vinegar, no eruption, am I right?" Aretha asked. I thought I saw a smile behind her serious expression. This was probably the best thing that had happened to her all day.

"You're right," I said glumly.

The judges were one table away. We were doomed.

Aretha turned to Roland. "Hand me some lemon juice."

Roland handed her a big green bottle of lemon juice. Aretha handed it to me.

"I don't know if it will work as well as vinegar, but it should have some reaction with the baking soda. Just use a ton."

"Do you have enough?" I asked her.

"I was the one in charge of bringing our supplies," she told me.

That meant they had enough.

"Okay, guys, tell us what you've got here," Mrs. Patino said, standing in front of our table.

So we told her. We told her about volcanoes, and we told her about the time period when dinosaurs and volcanoes coexisted, and we told her about the Ring of Fire.

Well, mostly I told her. Ben mostly moved the dinosaurs around to make it seem like a live-action science project.

And then, when we were done telling the judges all the many interesting facts about volcanoes, I dumped half a box of baking soda and half a bottle of dish-washing liquid into the volcano. Some of the stuff didn't actually make it all the way into the volcano, but I pretended like I'd done that on purpose.

Then I poured on the lemon juice.

And waited.

I poured some more.

And waited.

Okay, so our science project was a bust. I looked down at my feet.

My scientific career at Woodbrook Elementary School was over.

And then it happened.

Our volcano erupted.

All around us people started clapping and whistling. Including the judges.

Including Aretha Timmons.

Honorable
Mention

chapter fifteen

Our volcano didn't win first place in the fourth-grade science fair.

It didn't win second or third place either.

It did win an honorable mention, along with five other projects.

Ben wore the honorable-mention ribbon pinned to his shirt to school the next day. "It's the first ribbon I ever won," he said when I told him it wasn't like an Olympic medal or anything.

"Didn't you ever win a prize for your art?" I told him.

Ben looked sad. "No, I told you, I'm not really allowed to be an artist. Art's for girls."

Just then a pencil popped down so hard on Ben's desk I thought it was going to pop straight through to the other side.

"You talk too much about what's for girls and what's for boys and which side is smarter and a whole bunch of other stupid stuff," Aretha said, glaring at Ben. "Girls can do anything they want, and boys can do anything they want."

Ben's face brightened. "Maybe I could be a scientific artist. Like somebody who illustrates science books for schools or something."

"Who says you can't be a regular, everyday sort of artist?" Aretha asked.

"My dad."

Aretha shook her head. "You know what my dad says? When it's time to sign up for the band in sixth grade, I can only play flute or clarinet. You know what instrument I'm going to play?"

"Flute or clarinet?" Ben said.

"No, I'm going to play the trombone," Aretha told him. "Because I am a natural born trombone player, just like Mac here is a natural born scientist and you are a natural born artist."

"But what about your dad?" Ben asked.

Aretha folded her arms across her chest. "He will have to learn to live with it."

Ben looked as if making your dad learn to live with something was a new idea to him.

He looked as if it was an idea he liked.

"Anyway," Aretha said, sitting down in her desk. "I already have a great idea for next year's science fair. But I'll need your help. Both of you."

Did I mention that Aretha and Roland won second place in the fourth-grade science fair? The tape recorder kid got first prize.

"Here's a folder for you and one for you," she said, handing me and Ben each a red binder. "Inside you'll find some notes I made last night at the dinner table. You should ignore the spaghetti sauce stains."

At lunch Ben, Aretha, and I all sat together and talked about scientific stuff and comic-book stuff and compared allergies. Ben, it turns out, is allergic to poison ivy, poison oak, and poison sumac, which he found out at camp last summer. Aretha is allergic to eggs, so she has spent a lot of her spare time inventing egg-free cookie recipes.

When I told them my list of everything I'm allergic to, I left off the part about girls. Aretha didn't believe that it was possible to be allergic to purple. Ben pulled a purple pen out of his backpack and drew a picture of Derek the Destroyer on my arm. Little red spots popped up all around it.

"See, I'm not kidding," I said. "I really am allergic to purple."

"It's all in your head, Mac," Aretha said. "That's the only explanation."

"Maybe," I said.

And then my arm started itching really, really bad. But Ben wouldn't let me scratch it because he didn't want me to mess up his picture, and Aretha wouldn't let me scratch it because she wanted to take some scientific notes about my hives.

I would never get in the way of somebody taking scientific notes. So I sat there a long time, until I thought my arm might fall off from the itchiness.

In case you were wondering, it didn't. But it might next time.

Which, you have to admit, would be sort of cool.

Scientifically speaking.

MAC'S SCIENCE EXPERIMENTS

A VERY SIMPLE VOLCANO

What you'll need:

2-liter soda bottle
1/4 cup dishwashing liquid
about 6 drops of red food coloring
1/4 cup baking soda
1/2 cup vinegar or lemon juice

How to do it:

Set the bottle in a roasting pan. Pour in the dishwashing liquid, food coloring, baking soda (you could use a funnel to pour in the baking soda, if you've got one handy), and vinegar. Then stand back and wait for your volcano to erupt!

Note: If the lava isn't actually making its way out of the bottle, pour in some water to get it flowing.

So what happened?

When you mix baking soda and vinegar, you create carbon dioxide, the same gas you'll find in a real, live volcano. The gas bubbles build up in the bottle and force out the soapy lava mix.

MICROWAVE MARSHMALLOW ROAST

What you'll need:

2 jumbo-size marshmallows
a paper plate
a microwave oven

How to do it:

Place the marshmallows on the paper plate, and place the plate in the microwave with the help of a grown-up. Nuke the marshmallows for thirty seconds on high and watch as the marshmallows grow humongous. Remove the marshmallows and let them cool before touching them. Notice that as they cool, they start to deflate. They get really hard and yucky. You definitely don't want to eat them.

So what happened?

The water in the marshmallows was heated up by the microwave. This, in turn, warmed up and softened the sugar in the marshmallows. Energy (heat) from the water molecules also heated up the air bubbles in the marshmallows, making the air bubbles move faster and caused the walls of the marshmallows to expand. When the marshmallows cooled, the air bubbles shrank and the sugar hardened.

EXPLODING FILM CANISTERS

What you'll need:

sunglasses or safety goggles
half a tab of Alka-Seltzer
an empty 35-mm film canister with its lid
Water

How to do it:

Put on your sunglasses or safety goggles, then place the Alka-Seltzer tab in the film canister. Fill the canister halfway up with water. Place the lid on the canister and toss the canister on the ground, at least ten feet away from where you're standing. Watch with glee as the whole thing goes flying in the air.

So what happened?

The gas pressure created by the Alka-Seltzer tablet as it dissolved forced the lid off the film canister and sent it flying into the air.